The Ladybird Key Words Reading Scheme is based on these commonly used words. Those used most often in the English language are introduced first — with other words of popular appeal to children. All the Key Words list is covered in the early books, and the later titles use further word lists to develop full reading fluency. The total number of different words which will be learned in the complete reading scheme is nearly two thousand. The gradual introduction of these words, frequent repetition and complete 'carry-over' from book to book, will ensure rapid learning.

The full colour illustrations have been designed to create a desirable attitude towards learning — by making every child *eager* to read each title. Thus this attractive reading scheme embraces not only the latest findings in word frequency, but also the natural interests and activities of happy children.

Each book contains a list of the new words introduced.

W MURRAY, the author of the Ladybird Key Words Reading Scheme, is an experienced headmaster, author and lecturer on the teaching of reading. He is co-author, with J McNally, of Key Words to Literacy — *a teacher's book published by The Teacher Publishing Co Ltd.*

THE LADYBIRD KEY WORDS READING SCHEME has 12 graded books in each of its three series — 'a', 'b' and 'c'. As explained in the handbook *Teaching Reading*, these 36 graded books are all written on a controlled vocabulary, and take the learner from the earliest stages of reading to reading fluency.

The 'a' series gradually introduces and repeats new words. The parallel 'b' series gives the needed further repetition of these words at each stage, but in a different context and with different illustrations.

The 'c' series is also parallel to the 'a' series, and supplies the necessary link with writing and phonic training.

An illustrated booklet — *Notes for using the Ladybird Key Words Reading Scheme* — can be obtained free from the publishers. This booklet fully explains the Key Words principle. It also includes information on the reading books, work books and apparatus available, and such details as the vocabulary loading and reading ages of all books.

BOOK 1c
The Ladybird Key Words Reading Scheme

Read and write

by W MURRAY

with illustrations by
J H WINGFIELD

Ladybird Books Loughborough

After reading Books 1a and 1b the learner should copy out and complete the following pages in an exercise book. Answers are given on Pages 46 to 51 for corrections, revision and testing.

Here is Peter.

I like P____.

The answer is on Page 46

Here is Jane.

I like J_ _ _.

The answer is on Page 46

Here is a dog.

I like the d__.

The answer is on Page 46

Here is a shop.

I like the s___.

The answer is on Page 46

Here is a ball.

I like the b___.

The answer is on Page 47

Here is a tree.

I like the t_ _ _.

Here is a toy.

I like the t _ _ .

The answer is on Page 47

The s _ _ _ is here.

The t _ _ _ is here.

The answers are on Page 47

The d_ _ is here.

The b_ _ _ is here.

The answers are on Page 48

1 Peter and Jane
like t _ _ d _ _ .

2 The dog likes
t _ _ b _ _ _ .

The answers are on Page 48

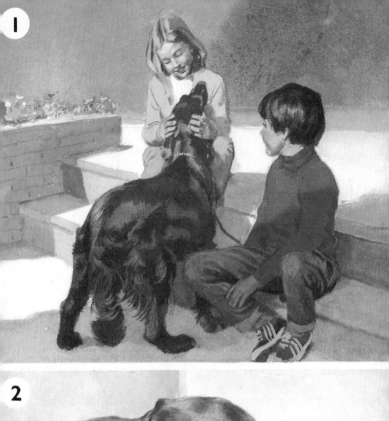

Yes   No

Is Peter here? ___.

Is Jane here? ___.

Is the dog here? __.

The answers are on Page 48

Yes   No

Is Peter in the shop? __.

Is Jane in the shop? ___.

Is the dog in the shop? __.

The answers are on Page 48

Yes   No

Has Jane a
toy? ___.

Has Peter a
toy? ___.

Has the dog a
ball? __.

The answers are on Page 49

Peter writes.

Peter likes to write.

I like t_ w____.

The answer is on Page 49

Jane writes.

Jane likes to write.

I like t_ w_ _ _ _.

The answer is on Page 49

1 Peter is in the s_ _ _.

The dog is
i_ the shop.

2 The ball is
i_ the tree.

Jane is i_ the tree.

The answers are on Page 50

1 I like t_ _ _ _.

2 I like t_ _ _.

3 I like P_ _ _ _ and
J_ _ _.

4 I like d_ _ _.

The answers are on Page 50

1 trees

2 toys

3 Peter and Jane

4 dogs

1 Jane has t-- d--.

2 Peter has - b----.

3 The dog h-- a ball.

4 The shop h-- toys.

The answers are on Page 50

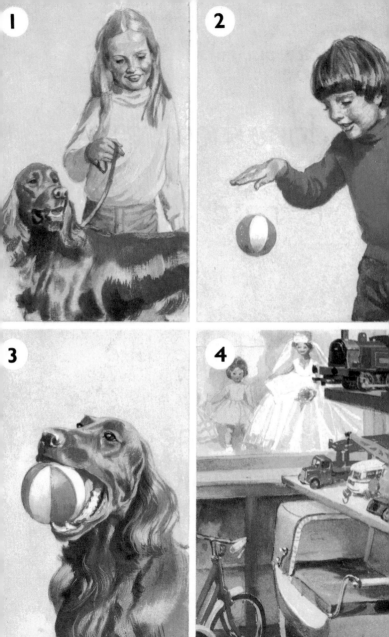

Write out correctly—

1 Jane here is.

2 is here Peter.

3 dog I the like.

4 Peter Jane and dog like the.

The answers are on Page 51
The use of flash cards may be helpful with these exercises.

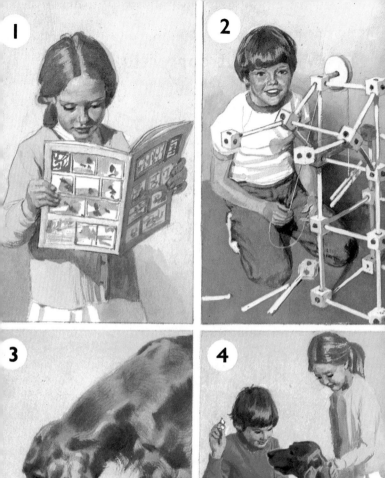
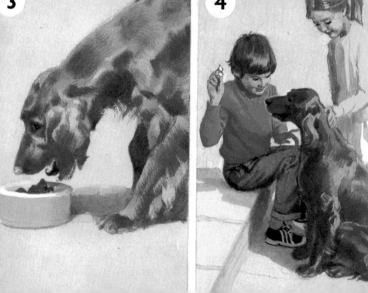

Write out correctly—

1 Here toy a is.

2 tree Here is a.

3 like toys I.

4 tree a in toy a is Here.

The answers are on Page 51
The use of flash cards may be helpful with these exercises.